Postman Pat®

ANNUAL 2006

This Postman Pat Annual
belongs to

....

Contents

Written and edited by Brenda Apsley
Designed by Graham Wise

EGMONT
We bring stories to life
Published in Great Britain in 2005 by Egmont Books Ltd,
239 Kensington High Street, London W8 6SA.
Printed in Italy   ISBN 1 4052 2106 2
10 9 8 7 6 5 4 3 2

Hello,

My name is Pat Clifton, but everyone calls me **Postman Pat** because I'm the Greendale village postman!

Greendale is a very friendly place and I know everyone because it's my job to deliver the post each day. People are used to seeing me driving around in my little red van with my cat **Jess**.

This year has been a busy one and you can read all about it in my new annual. I hope you like it!

Say Hello to Postman Pat and His Family

Pat Clifton is the Greendale postman. He lives on the edge of the village in a house called Forge Cottage. Pat always has a smile on his face because he enjoys delivering the post to his friends and neighbours. He's always ready to stop for a chat, to share a joke or to help them with a problem.

Pat is married to **Sara**. They met when she was working for the Post Office. Now she works in the Greendale Light Railway station café. Sara loves baking and her cakes usually win prizes at the Pencaster Show.

Pat and Sara's son is called **Julian**. You can find out all about him on page 15.

8

One very important member of the Clifton family is **Jess**, Pat's black and white cat. He goes everywhere with Pat. Jess loves exploring all sorts of things, which sometimes gets him – and Pat – into scrapes. Jess loves eating fish and chasing mice.

Jess hasn't managed to catch one yet!

Colour in this picture of Pat and his family.

Say Hello to Postman Pat's Friends and Neighbours

Mrs Goggins lives at the Post Office in the High Street. She works there, too, selling stamps and sorting out all the letters and parcels for Pat to deliver.

Dorothy and Alf Thompson live on a small farm called Thompson Ground where they keep their animals including goats, pigs and hens. They make goats' cheeses and grow vegetables to sell on their stall at the market in Pencaster.

Reverend Peter Timms is the vicar of Greendale. He lives in a house beside the church, right in the centre of the village. He's funny and kind and everyone likes him.

Doctor Sylvia Gilbertson is in charge of the Greendale medical clinic. She's firm but kind and works very hard because it's her job to look after everyone in Greendale.

PC Arthur Selby is Greendale's policeman. He rides around the village on his bicycle, checking that the roads are safe and sorting out traffic jams.

Ted Glen lives at Black Moss Cottage. He's the local handyman and he can fix anything from a leaky roof to a broken clock. He helps out at the railway, too.

Julia Pottage has a large farm just outside the village called Greendale Farm. She's a very good farmer and keeps lots of sheep, and a herd of cows for milk.

Can you point to Pat and his friends, and say their names?

All About the Greendale Light Railway

The **Greendale Light Railway** is quite close to the village green. An old steam engine called the Greendale Rocket takes passengers and post between the village station and Pencaster, the local town.

Ajay Bains looks after the railway. He's the station master and the driver and he makes sure everything is clean and tidy. He loves old steam engines and knows everything there is to know about them so looking after the Greendale Rocket is his ideal job.

Nisha Bains is married to Ajay. She sells tickets for the train and works in the station café with Sara. The café is not just for passengers — lots of villagers call in for one of Sara's cakes, a cup of tea and a chat.

Meera Bains is seven years old. You can find out about her on page 14.

Nikhil is the youngest member of the Bains family. He's just six months old and he's a happy, cheerful baby who is always smiling. Everyone calls him Nik.

All About Greendale Primary School

The village school is called Greendale Primary. It's small and has just one teacher, Jeff Pringle. His pupils like him because he always tries to make learning fun. Here are Mr Pringle's pupils.

Charlie Pringle is seven. He's Mr Pringle's son and he's very clever. He loves computers and science and has lots of hobbies and interests.

Meera Bains has just moved to Greendale from Pencaster. She loves the countryside so she's very happy in the village and has made lots of new friends.

Lucy Selby is the Greendale policeman's daughter. She's seven and likes doing quiet things like reading, dressing up and playing let's-pretend games.

14

Bill Thompson is the oldest pupil at the school. He's nine and when he grows up he wants to be a farmer, just like his dad. He likes helping out on the family farm, Thompson Ground.

Sarah Gilbertson, Lucy's best friend, is the doctor's daughter. She's eight years old and much noisier than Lucy. She's a real chatterbox! She loves riding her pony, Snowbella.

Julian Clifton is Pat and Sara's son. He's six and he loves playing sport and watching his favourite football team, Pencaster United. Meera Bains used to be his pen friend before she moved to Greendale.

Katy and **Tom Pottage** are six-year-old twins who live at Greendale Farm with their mum. Katy is a few minutes older than her brother and she can be a bit bossy. But Tom doesn't mind – he's happy to follow his sister anywhere.

Postman Pat and the Butterflies

1 It was a very windy day in Greendale. Leaves and bits of paper blew around and Julia Pottage had to hold on to her new hat to stop it blowing away.

"That's a lovely hat, Julia," said Dorothy Thompson, who was wearing her old scarf. "Oh, I'd really love a new hat," she said to herself.

2 When Postman Pat passed by the school he showed Jess a flower. But when Jess went to sniff it – it flew away! **"Meow!"** said Jess.

Inside, Mr Pringle showed the pupils a picture. "Two butterflies have gone missing from the zoo," he said. "There's a reward for whoever finds them."

3 "You can look for them this afternoon," said Mr Pringle. "But if you find them be gentle, because butterflies are very delicate."

Back at Thompson Ground Dorothy found an old brown hat. It looked very plain – until she pinned a bunch of cherries to it! "There!" she said. "That's better!"

4 Later on the children went to look for the butterflies. They had special nets to catch them in. **"Sssh!"** said Bill, leading the way. **"Follow me!"** The children didn't see the butterflies, who fluttered around the village then flew off to Thompson Ground – and landed on Dorothy's new hat!

5 When Pat arrived with the post he looked hard at Dorothy's hat. "You know, I'm sure I've seen that flower before," he said.

"Meow!" Jess thought so too!

Back in Greendale the children were still searching for the butterflies. When Bill saw one over the hedge he flipped his net over it. "Got it!" he said.

6 "Oh!" said Nisha Bains. "What are you doing?" The butterfly wasn't a real one – it was a toy one that was attached to baby Nikhil's buggy.

Later on Pat met PC Selby outside the school. "Come and look at this flower, Arthur," said Pat. "I've never seen one quite like it before."

7 But the flower had gone! "That's a pity. You know, it was just like one on Dorothy's hat," said Pat.

"I hope she didn't pick it!" said PC Selby.

In the Post Office Mrs Goggins told Dorothy how much she liked all the bright colours on her hat. Dorothy was puzzled. The cherries were all red!

8 PC Selby saw Dorothy and jumped off his bike to look at her hat. "You know you shouldn't pick wild flowers, don't you?" he said, pointing to the flower – which flew away!

Dorothy took her hat off. "What flowers?" she asked. "It's a bunch of cherries!"

19

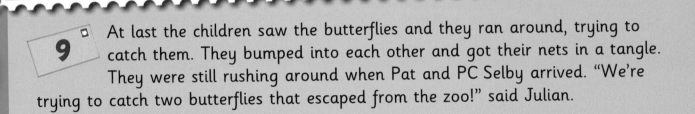

9 At last the children saw the butterflies and they ran around, trying to catch them. They bumped into each other and got their nets in a tangle. They were still rushing around when Pat and PC Selby arrived. "We're trying to catch two butterflies that escaped from the zoo!" said Julian.

10 While the chase was going on Dorothy sat on a bench with her back against a stone wall. Up flew the butterflies – and landed on her hat again! Pat saw them from the other side of the wall and borrowed Charlie's net. He lowered it over the butterflies – and Dorothy's head!

11 "What's going on, Pat?" asked Dorothy.

Pat took the net off her head and showed her the butterflies.

"They escaped from the zoo," said Pat. "Now what can we put them in?"

Dorothy took a storage box from her shopping bag. "I just bought this," she said, "but you can use it."

12 "Thanks, Dorothy," said Pat. "I'll make some holes in the lid so they can breathe then I'll take them back to the zoo."

Pat wasn't away for long and when he came back he had free tickets to the zoo for everyone.

"Hurray!" said Bill. "Three cheers for the butterflies!"

Read a Story with Postman Pat

You can read the butterfly story with me. When you see a picture, say the word.

When two escaped from

the zoo and his friends tried to

find them. "This way!" said  .

He caught one of the  but

it was a toy one on 's buggy!

When the  landed on 's

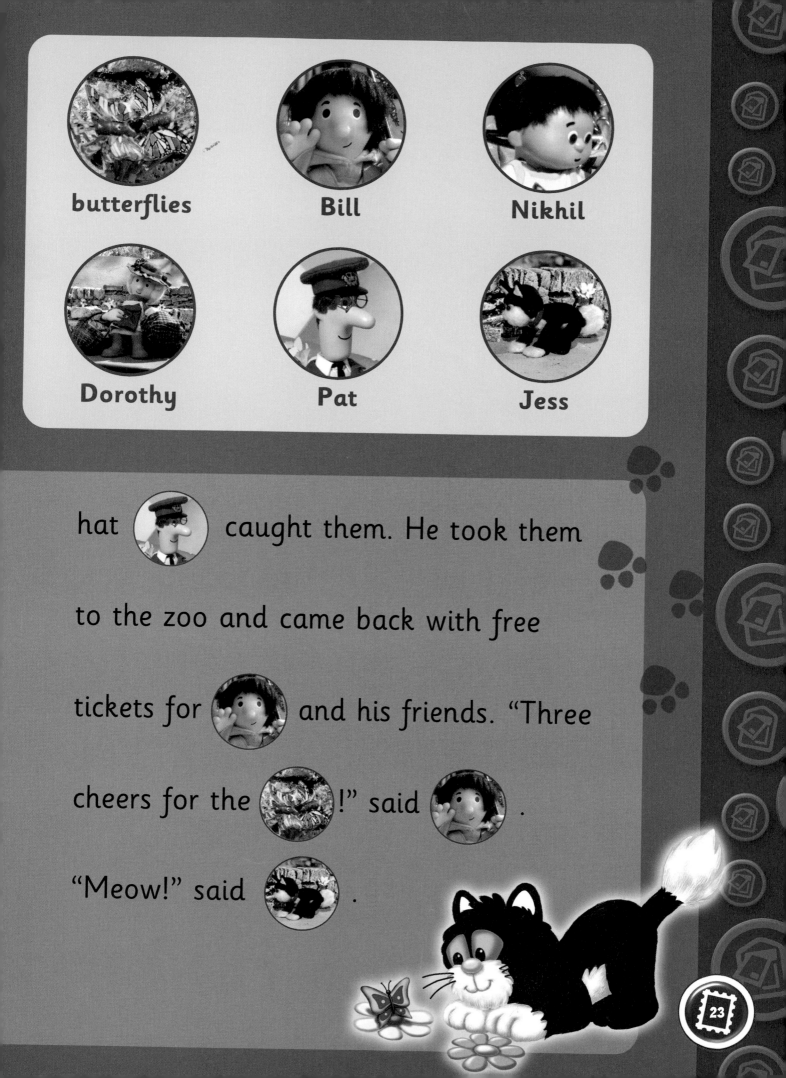

butterflies

Bill

Nikhil

Dorothy

Pat

Jess

hat caught them. He took them

to the zoo and came back with free

tickets for and his friends. "Three

cheers for the !" said .

"Meow!" said .

23

Count with Postman Pat

What a lot of butterflies!
Can you help me count them?
When you find a butterfly colour in a little one that matches it at the bottom of the page.
Count how many you've coloured and write numbers in the boxes.

25

Postman Pat Clowns Around

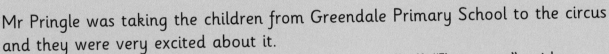

Mr Pringle was taking the children from Greendale Primary School to the circus and they were very excited about it.

But there was bad news. The circus was cancelled! "I'm sorry," said Mr Pringle. "Maybe we can go next year."

"Oh no!" said Bill Thompson. "Let's put on our own circus instead! Please? Can we?"

"Yes!" said Meera. "We can borrow my uncle's big tent."

Mr Pringle smiled. "All right then."

Next morning, Pat went to the railway station to pick up the tent.

"We'll load it into my van, Ajay," said Pat. "You take one end and I'll take the other." But the tent was too big to fit inside! "We'll just have to carry it to the village green," said Pat.

"Oh ... right," said Ajay.

The other villagers were on the village green when Pat and Ajay arrived – and they all knew just where the tent should go.

"Over there a bit."

"This way."

"No, that way."

"Right a bit."

"Left a bit."

"Back a bit."

"Forward a bit."

"Turn it round."

"No, the other way."

By the time Pat and Ajay moved the tent to just the right place they were tired, out of breath – and a bit dizzy.

"Phew!" said Pat.

The children practised their circus skills.

Bill tried to show the girls how to do their ribbon dance but he ended up tying himself up in the ribbons!

Then Bill tried to show his other friends how to juggle with bean bags. But he threw them up too high and they landed on his head! **"Ouch!"**

Julian put some flowerpots on the ground. "Jess, I want you to jump from one to the other," he said. "Got it?"

"Meow!" said Jess.

But when he saw a butterfly Jess forgot what he was meant to be doing and ran after it.

"I'll help," said Bill. **"Jump, Jess!"**

Jess jumped from flowerpot to flowerpot – but then he jumped on Bill! **"Ouch!"**

Poor Bill — he still didn't have an act of his own.

He balanced a pile of books on his head, but they all fell off.

Pat smiled. "You do make me laugh, Bill!" he said.

"But I want to be good at something," said Bill. "I'm no good at anything. People just laugh at me."

"But it's good to make people laugh!" said Pat. "Clowns make people laugh, don't they?"

That gave Bill an idea. "I'll be a clown!" he said. "But not on my own."

"Then we'll both be clowns," said Pat. "Come on, let's practise."

On the day of the circus the big tent was filled with bright lights and music.

The ring master, Mr Pringle, said "Welcome to the Greendale circus!" and the bean-bag jugglers performed their act.

Then it was the turn of the ribbon dancers. They looked lovely!

Next, Jess did his act perfectly.

"**Great!**" said Julian.

"**Meow!**" said Jess.

Last of all came the clowns, Pat and Bill. First Bill squirted Pat with a water pistol hidden in a flower.

Then Pat slipped on a banana skin and landed on his bottom: **"Oof!"**

At the end of their act Bill and Pat pretended to throw buckets of water at the crowd — but they were filled with confetti, not water!

The clowns were the stars of the show. They made everyone laugh and when they took a bow there were extra-loud claps and cheers.

"Hurray!" cried the audience. **"More!"**

There was a big parade around the ring at the end of the show.

"Didn't they all do well?" said Mr Pringle proudly. "It proves that everyone is good at something."

Pat smiled at Bill. "He's right you know," he whispered. **"Well done, Bill!"**

Jigsaw Puzzle Pictures

Pat and Julian like doing jigsaw puzzles. Can you help them find the 2 pieces that will fit into the spaces and complete each jigsaw picture? You can draw and colour in the pieces if you like.

1.

a.

b.

c.

d.

e.

a.

b.

c.

d.

e.

2.

Postman Pat and the Greendale Movie

1 One morning Mrs Goggins gave Pat a parcel. "It's my new video camera," said Pat. "Smile please, Mrs Goggins!"
Mrs Goggins shook her head. "Don't film me!" she said. "Why don't you make a film of Greendale instead?"

2 Pat smiled. "That's a great idea," he said. "I'll show my film at the school hall tonight. Will you tell everyone about it?"
Mrs Goggins nodded.
Pat wasn't sure how the video camera worked so he read the instructions. "Now how do I switch this thing on?" he asked.
Jess seemed to know:

"Meow!"

3 Pat's first delivery was at the church. He was filming Reverend Timms playing the piano when he remembered the post, so he left his camera on the font while he went to get it.

When Pat got back the vicar was hot and out of breath. He'd been playing rock and roll, not hymns!

4 At the railway station Ajay and Ted were busy cleaning the Greendale Rocket.

"How does that thing work?" Ted asked.

"It's just a matter of pressing the right button," said Pat.

But Ted wanted to try for himself and he grabbed the camera.

"Careful!" said Pat. **"Watch out!"**

But it was too late. Pat's letters flew up into the air and he had to put his camera down so that he could run along the platform to collect them.

When he got back, Ajay had a bucket of soapy water on his head!

"Shall I film you now?" laughed Pat.

"Er, no," said Ajay. "Not just now."

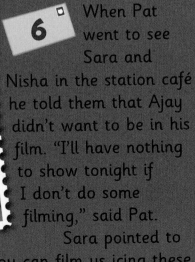

6 When Pat went to see Sara and Nisha in the station café he told them that Ajay didn't want to be in his film. "I'll have nothing to show tonight if I don't do some filming," said Pat.

Sara pointed to some cakes. "You can film us icing these cakes if you like," she said.

7 Pat was filming them when — **CRASH!** — Jess knocked a plate off a table. There was cake all over the floor. "I'll clean it up," said Pat, putting his camera down.

When he looked up again Sara and Nisha were covered in icing!

"What happened?" asked Pat.

"Er ... nothing ..." said Sara.

 8 That night everyone went to the school hall to watch Pat's film. "I haven't seen it myself yet," said Pat, "but I hope you enjoy it."

Ted switched off the lights, Pat pressed a button — and Mrs Goggins' face appeared on the screen. **"I don't remember that bit ..."** said Pat.

9 When Reverend Timms came on screen playing rock and roll, everyone laughed. **"I don't remember filming that bit!"** said Pat. The next face filled the whole screen. It was Jess, with his nose pressed up against the camera lens! **"I'm sure I didn't film that!"** said Pat.

10 When the film showed Ajay picking up a bucket of water instead of a letter, Pat said, **"So that's what happened!"**

The audience was still laughing at Ajay and Ted when the film showed Sara and Nisha's bags of icing splitting and spattering all over their faces.

11 "I'm really sorry everyone," said Pat. "This isn't what I was expecting to see. The camera must have been running when I wasn't there."

Ted smiled. "You don't have to apologise, Pat," he said. "That film is the funniest thing I've ever seen." The others all seemed to agree.

12 "You mean you liked it? You really liked it?" said Pat.

"Yes, we all loved it," said Julian as everyone clapped and cheered. "I think you're the best film director ever, Dad!" he said proudly.

Jess agreed with him. "Meow!" he said. "MEOW!"

The Greendale Movie Picture Puzzle

Look carefully! Which of the little pictures can you see in the big ones? Write a tick (✔) for 'yes in the big picture' or a cross (✗) for 'not in the big picture'.

1.

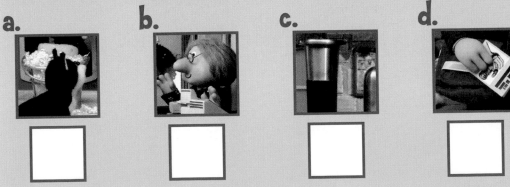

a.   b.   c.   d.

a.

b.

c.

d.

ANSWERS: stamp 1, pictures a and c; stamp 2, pictures b and c.

A Year in Greendale

Greendale is a lovely place to live in whatever the season of the year.

In **spring** Julia Pottage waters the flowers in her garden tub.

Sara Gilbertson loves **summer** because she can play outside all day.

Autumn is rainy and windy and Jess doesn't like getting his paws wet – so Pat gives him a ride.

Winter is cold and snowy but Postman Pat still takes the post to Thompson Ground.

Colour in the pictures of Greendale through the year then write your name on the line below.

A year in **Greendale** by _____

Postman Pat at the Seaside

1 It was the school holidays and at the station Meera was a bit fed up.
"I've got something that will cheer you up," said Pat. "I've got a postcard for you."

Meera read the message. "It's from cousin Sanjay!" she said. "He's on holiday at the seaside. Oh, can we go, Mum, can we?"

2 Ted was driving past the village green with a load of sand on the back of his lorry when he went over a big bump. The tailboard came undone and all the sand poured out on to the ground. It was all over the grass! Ted stopped the lorry and looked at it.

3 "That's torn it!" said Ted. "What am I going to do?"

He was still wondering what to do about the sand when PC Selby arrived on his bike. "That sand can't stay there, Ted," he said, using his hat to scoop up some sand.

Ted sighed. "This is going to take all day!"

4 When Pat drove to the village green and saw the sand he stopped to help. "We've got to move all this sand," Ted explained.

"You need something to load it into," said Pat. "But what?"

Jess knew! **"Meow!"** He jumped out of Pat's van with some empty mailbags.

"Good idea!" said Pat.

5 Back at the station Meera asked her dad why they couldn't go to the seaside.

"It's too far away for a day trip," said Ajay. "And who needs the seaside anyway? Let's have a day out in Greendale instead. We'll take a picnic with us. Come on, let's go."

6 PC Selby and Ted used their hats to scoop sand into the mailbags but it ran through the gaps in the cloth. Then Pat had an idea. He borrowed a wheelbarrow and they filled it with sand. But when Pat wheeled it up a plank on to Ted's lorry it wobbled and fell off!

7 Ajay and his family walked to Thompson Ground and laid out their picnic. Suddenly they heard a loud buzz-buzzing noise. "What's that?" asked Meera.

It was Dorothy Thompson's bees! "Why don't you have your picnic at Greendale Farm instead?" she said.

8 Pat heard a noise too. "That's Doctor Gilbertson's big vacuum cleaner," said Pat. "We'll use it to suck up the sand then blow it into the lorry."

The cleaner sucked up the sand and the bag got **bigger** ... and **bigger** – but then it **burst!** Pat and the others were covered in sand.

9 At Greendale Farm Ajay and Nisha laid out the picnic again. But they weren't the only ones in the field!

"**Baaaa!**" They were surrounded by sheep! When one of them snatched Ajay's sandwich he tried to shoo them away but they didn't want to go. "We may as well go home," said Meera.

10 Pat and the others were still trying to get rid of the sand when Julian and his friends arrived – with buckets and spades! "When I saw all this sand it gave me an idea," said Julian. "It's just like the seaside! Come on – dig in!"

Jess thought that was a great idea: "**Meow!**"

11 The Bains family were on their way home when Meera heard excited voices and music coming from the village green. It had been turned into a seaside beach, with sandcastles and deckchairs and even a paddling pool.

"What do you think of **Greendale-on-Sea?**" asked Pat.

12 "You wanted to go to the seaside didn't you, Meera?" said Pat. "Well this is the next best thing. You couldn't go to the seaside so we've brought the seaside to you."

Meera grinned. "Thank you, Postman Pat," she said. "This is the best day out **ever!**"

Read a Story with Postman Pat

You can read the Greendale-on-Sea story with me. When you see a picture, say the word, using the key on the right.

 wanted to go to the seaside.

"It's too far," said . "We'll have a picnic instead." But some noisy bees and lots of hungry spoiled it.

"This isn't much fun," said .

"Sorry," said . "We may as well go home," said .

Meera Ajay sheep Ted

Pat PC Selby Julian

When lots of sand fell off Ted 's lorry

Pat and PC Selby tried to get rid of it.

But Julian and his friends had a better

idea! They made the sand into a beach!

"Welcome to Greendale-on-Sea!" said

Pat and Ajay smiled. "This is

the best day out ever!" said Meera .

olouring Fun

On Christmas Day, Dad and I get up extra early to decorate the Christmas tree.

Draw a big star on top of the tree then colour in the picture as neatly as you can.

Would you like to draw your own picture of Jess?
It's easy if you copy the lines square by square.

Now colour in your drawing and write your name on the line below.

Jess by _____

Postman Pat the Magician

One morning Mrs Goggins and Postman Pat were busy sorting out the post.

"There's a lot for Meera," said Mrs Goggins.

"Yes, it's her birthday tomorrow," said Pat.

"And this parcel's for you, Pat," said Mrs Goggins.

"Oh good," said Pat, unwrapping a book called **The Big Book of Magic Tricks.** "I've promised to do some magic tricks at Meera's birthday party tomorrow."

When Pat went to the station with the post Meera was waiting for him. "I've got a lot of post for someone today," said Pat, handing over her birthday cards. "I wonder who?"

"ME!" said Meera. "Thank you, Pat. You're coming to my party aren't you? We're having lots of food and a disco. I wanted a magician to do tricks too, but Mum couldn't find one."

Nisha winked at Pat.

Pat winked at Nisha.

"Never mind," Pat said. "I'm sure it'll be a great party anyway."

Later on Pat showed Ted and Ajay the book of magic tricks.

"There's a trick called Levitation," said Pat. "It means making someone float up in the air. I'd need a big car-jack to lift them though."

"No problem," said Ted. "I've got one in the shed."

He turned a page in the book. "What about making someone disappear in a Box of Mystery, Pat? We can make one for you."

"That's great," said Pat. "I'm going to do some card tricks as well so I'd better go and practise."

When Pat got home Sara and Julian were busy making his magician's outfit. Jess wanted to help too but he ended up covered in blobs of black paint and bits of glitter! **"Meow!"**

Pat read his magic book then he held out some cards to Julian. "Take a card then put it back," said Pat, shuffling the cards. "Your card was – the two of spades."

"No it wasn't," said Julian.

Poor Pat! Doing magic tricks was much harder than it looked!

Next morning Pat went to look at Ajay and Ted's Levitation machine. Jess climbed on to a little platform, Ajay moved a lever — and Jess went up into the air!

"Meow!" said Jess.

"Brilliant!" said Pat.

Ted showed Pat the Box of Mystery. Jess jumped inside then Pat closed the curtain. Jess jumped out of a flap at the back and Pat opened the curtain again. The box was empty!

"Da-darrr!" said Pat. "Jess has disappeared!"

Pat closed the curtain again. But Jess didn't want to get back in — until Ajay tempted him in with one of his sandwiches!

When Pat opened the curtain again there he was!

"Da-darrr!" said Pat. "Jess is back again!"

Meera's party was a great success. After the food and dancing, there was a special surprise for her — a magician called the Great Patini, and his assistant, Nisha!

Patini turned his magic wand into a bunch of flowers then produced a necklace for Meera. Patini knew just which card Lucy had chosen and the audience clapped and cheered.

Next, Patini asked Meera to lie on his magic table. Then he waved his wand and said:

"With this magic you shall fly
Higher up towards the sky!"

The audience gasped as Meera went up into the air then down again. It really was magic!

Patini's next trick was the Box of Mystery.

Jess jumped inside then went out of the back flap when Patini closed the red curtains.

"Da-darrrr!" said Patini as he opened the curtains. "Jess has disappeared!"

Patini closed the curtains again and Meera used a chicken leg to tempt Jess to go back into the box again. But Jess ran off with the chicken leg and when Patini opened the curtains again the box was empty!

"Da ..." said Patini. "Now where's he gone?"

Ted knew, and he whispered to Patini.

Patini smiled and went over to the table where he had put his top hat. He waved his wand, said,

**"Jess is white and Jess is black.
I command you, Jess – come back!"**

– and up popped Jess!

"Meow!" said Jess.

It was a great trick and the audience clapped and cheered.

"How did you do that, Dad?" asked Julian later.

Pat winked. "Easy," he said. "It's magic!"

"And so is my birthday party!" said Meera.

Picture Puzzles

Here are lots of pictures of Jess. They look the same — but are they? If you look carefully you'll see that one is different from the rest. Can you point to the odd one out?

1.

2.

3.

4.

5.

6.

7.

8.

I've taken lots of photographs of the Greendale Rocket. Can you find two that are exactly the same?

Postman Pat and the Great Greendale Race

One morning Postman Pat emptied the last letter from the postbox and put it into his sack.

He looked around. The sun was shining and the birds were singing. "There's nothing like a peaceful day in the country is there, Jess?" he said.

But before Jess could reply — **BRRRRRM!** — a noisy motorbike roared past.

It was Ajay!

Pat turned to Jess as Ajay disappeared in a cloud of dust. "Just think how quickly I'd get my round done if I went as fast as that," said Pat.

"**Meow!**" said Jess.

Later on Pat delivered a seed catalogue to Alf Thompson.
"Lovely day isn't it?" said Pat. "I was just saying how peaceful it ..."
BRRRRRM!

Ted's big noisy lorry rumbled past.

Alf watched it go. "That lorry of Ted's might be fast, but it's not as good as my old tractor. It never lets me down."

"Yes," said Pat. "I wouldn't swap my old post van for ... hey, I've got an idea, Alf. Why don't we have a race to see whose vehicle is the best?"

"You can count me in," said Alf.

"Right," said Pat. "I'll get it organised."

At Greendale Farm Pat told Julia Pottage about the race. "Why don't you have some tests for the drivers as well?" she suggested.

"Great idea!" said Pat. "Will you organise them?"

On the day of the Great Greendale Race Mr Pringle lined up the contestants on the starting line. Then he said, "Ready ... get set ... GO!" and they were off!

All except poor PC Selby, who had to pump up a flat tyre on his bike.

Ajay took the lead on his motorbike. Alf was next but his tractor was very slow. "Get a move on!" shouted Ted, who was behind him.

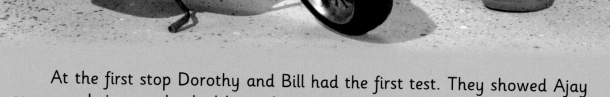

At the first stop Dorothy and Bill had the first test. They showed Ajay some road signs and asked him what they meant.

Ajay got them all right and zoomed off again.

Pat and Alf got to the crossroads at the same time.

"Which way?" said Alf.

"I'm going **THiS** way," said Pat.

"No, I reckon it's **THiS** way," said Alf.

They set off in opposite directions and drove around — until Alf came to another crossroads — and so did Pat!

"Looks like we **both** took the wrong road," said Pat. "So it must be this one. Come on."

Back at the start Mr Pringle was using his binoculars to let everyone know how the race was going. "It's Ajay in the lead, then Ted, Pat and Alf," he said.

"Where's my dad?" said Lucy.

At the second test Katy and Tom Pottage showed Ted some red, orange and green balls and asked him what the traffic light colours meant.

Ted knew them all, but he couldn't resist juggling with the balls.

When he dropped them they rolled under some blackberry bushes and by the time he had found them — and taken the prickly thorns from his fingers — PC Selby had passed him!

Alf was doing well when some sheep blocked his way. He was herding them back into their field when Pat arrived. **"Go on, Pat!"** said Alf. "You carry on!"

Soon Pat was at stop number three where Doctor Gilbertson was going to test his eyes.

Sarah held up a picture and Pat had to say what it was. But it was a LONG way away.

"Could be a teddy ... or a dog ..." said Pat.

"Meow!" said Jess. **"MEOW!"**

That was just the clue Pat needed!

"It's Jess!" he said.

Pat set off again but he stopped when he saw Ajay at the side of the road. He had run out of petrol. **"Get going,"** said Ajay. "The winning line is just around the corner."

"That doesn't matter," said Pat. "I've got a can of petrol in the van."

He was looking for it when PC Selby cycled past – and was first to cross the finishing line!

"PC Selby wins the race and Alf is second," said Mr Pringle. "Ted is third, Ajay fourth, and last of all is Postman Pat."

Reverend Timms presented PC Selby with the Greendale Cup – but there was a prize for Pat, too!

"This is a special prize for stopping to help Ajay and losing your chance of winning the race," said Reverend Timms, handing Pat one of Julia's famous apple pies.

"Thanks," said Pat. "Anyone for apple pie?"

"Yes please, Dad," said Julian. "But make sure you **WIN** next time will you?"

"Meow!" said Jess.

67

Postman Pat's Busy Week

I'm always busy because it's my job to make sure all the people in Greendale get their letters and parcels. Why not colour in the pictures of my busy week?

On **Monday** Sarah posts a birthday card to her friend Lucy. Pat delivers it the next morning.

On **Tuesday** Pat takes some seeds to Alf Thompson at Thompson Ground.

There's a new computer game for Charlie on **Wednesday**.

Nisha Bains is pleased when Pat delivers new tickets for the Greendale Light Railway on **Thursday**.

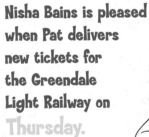

Pat takes a parcel to Ted Glen on **Friday.** It's his new spanner!

On **Saturday** Pat has a new story book for Mrs Goggins. Julian can't wait to hear it!

Sunday is Pat's day off!

Can you answer these questions about Postman Pat's busy week?
1. On which day did Pat take tickets to Nisha Bains?
2. Who posted a birthday card on Monday?
3. Who had some seeds delivered on Tuesday?
4. What did Pat deliver to Charlie on Wednesday?
5. On which day did Pat deliver Ted Glen's new spanner?

ANSWERS: 1. Thursday, 2. Sarah, 3. Alf Thompson, 4. a new computer game, 5. Friday.